CAMP BUCCANEER

CampBuccaneer

By PAM SMALLCOMB

Illustrated by
TOM LICHTENHELD

Aladdin Paperbacks
New York London Toronto Sydney Singapore

First Aladdin edition June 2002
Text copyright © 2002 by Pam Smallcomb
Illustrations copyright © 2002 by Tom Lichtenheld

ALADDIN PAPERBACKS
An imprint of Simon & Schuster Children's Publishing Division
1230 Avenue of the Americas, New York, NY 10020

Designed by Lisa Vega
The text of this book was set in Cooper Lt BT.

Printed in the United States of America
10 9 8 7 6 5 4 3 2 1

Library of Congress Cataloging-in-Publication Data
Smallcomb, Pam, 1954–
Camp Buccaneer / by Pam Smallcomb.
p. cm.
Summary: After spending summer vacation learning to be a real pirate at Camp Buccaneer, Marlon feels much better prepared to return to school and face Carla, the bully who has pestered her since kindergarten.
ISBN 0-689-84383-6 [lib.]
[1. Pirates—Fiction. 2. Interpersonal relations—Fiction. 3. Camps—Fiction. 4. Bullies—Fiction. 5. Schools—Fiction.] I. Title.
PZ7.S6375 Cam 2001
[Fic]—dc21
00-052230

To Rick and my mom and our six Buccaneers:

Chris, Amy, Alex, Caitlin, Patrick, and Lucas

CHAPTER ONE

"This place is *boring*," said Marlon. "But at least I'm far away from that awful Carla Axelrod."

Marlon's mom and dad had decided to rent a cabin on the lake for the summer.

Marlon said, "Now that we're away from EVERYTHING, what am I supposed to do?"

She looked at her dad. He was asleep on the couch. Strange sounds were coming from his mouth.

"Gross," said Marlon.

"Hmmm?" her mom said. "What did you say, dear?" She was reading a book. Marlon looked at the cover. It was one of those mushy books her mom loved.

"Nothing, Mom," Marlon said.

Marlon stared at the walls of the cabin.

"Well, you guys are really fun, but I need my exercise. I'm going for a walk," Marlon said.

"That's nice, dear," her mom said as she turned the page of her book.

As Marlon walked along, she thought about school. Then she thought about Carla Axelrod. Carla Axelrod was trying to ruin her life.

She had been in Marlon's class at school since kindergarten. And she always sat right behind Marlon.

"I bet she makes lists of mean things to do to me," thought Marlon. "And she probably has lots and lots of lists."

Carla Axelrod made fun of the way Marlon looked.

"Hey, look, it's Mackerel Face Marlon!" Carla yelled when Marlon got off the school bus.

Carla Axelrod made fun of her at recess.

"Don't pick Marlon," Carla said when they chose sides for soccer. "She messes up every time. She's Messed-up Marlon!"

Carla Axelrod made fun of her name.

"Hi, Moron, I mean Macaroon!" she said in the hall.

Marlon hadn't made any friends at school. Having Carla Axelrod in her class sure didn't help.

"Maybe this year will be better," she thought. "Maybe Carla Axelrod will move to Niagara Falls, or even China. Or maybe, just maybe, she won't be in my class just this once."

She thought of a whole year without Carla Axelrod tapping her on the back of the head with a pencil. That made Marlon smile.

Marlon reached the last cabin on the lake path. When she got closer, she heard singing:

"Buccaneer Bob and his seven smarmy mates
Set sail on the wide ocean blue. . . .
The sharks they got ol' Bob and ol' Bill,
And the other six died from the flu. . . ."

She tiptoed up to the porch. On the door was a sign that read:

CAMP BUCCANEER

Not FoR tHe FAiNt oF HeARt
LeARN to Be A CARD-CARRYiNG
PiRAte iN tHRee weeKs
◄ iNQUiRe witHiN ►

CHAPTER TWO

"Wow," said Marlon, "pirates!"

Marlon loved pirates. Every Halloween she dressed up like one. Even though every Halloween Carla Axelrod said pirates were stupid.

Marlon knocked on the door.

"Who be ye?" a voice bellowed from inside.

"My name is Marlon," she said. "I'd like to sign up for camp."

The door swung open. Marlon was face-to-face with a pirate. He was big. His beard was long and scraggy. A scar went from the tip of his nose to the bottom of his ear.

He was dirty. Marlon thought that he could use a nice bath with some of those perfumed soaps her mom kept by the bathroom sink.

"So," he sneered down at her, "ye think ye're made of pirate stuff, do ye? Ha! Ye're hardly big enough to swab a deck with. Be gone with ye!"

Marlon's face got red. She clenched her fists. "I'm big enough," she said. "And I'm pretty strong."

"Ye think so?" the pirate said. "Well, ye've got spunk. That'll serve ye well. Wait here and I'll get ye the papers. No one signs up fer Camp Buccaneer without first getting permission. Got to keep things on the up-and-up."

"Excuse me," said Marlon as she peeked inside. "What is *your* name?"

The pirate raised his right arm. At the end of his arm where his hand should be was a shiny silver hook. "They call me Shark Bait. That rascal got all five, he did." He laughed and walked inside.

"Cool," said Marlon.

She saw two more pirates inside. They were sitting on the floor, playing cards. "They be Peg Leg and William," Shark Bait said.

Shark Bait gave Marlon the papers. "Be sure yer parents read this and sign right there," Shark Bait said, stabbing the spot with his hook. "Camp starts tomorrow at six bells. Be sharp or ye'll walk the plank."

CHAPTER THREE

Marlon raced back to her cabin. "Mom, Dad, can I go to Camp Buccaneer? It's right here at the lake! All you have to do is sign these papers!" Marlon shoved them under her mother's nose.

"Well, I don't see why not. Won't it be nice for you to meet other children?" her mom said. She signed the papers with one hand. She turned the page of her book with the other.

"Is it all right with you, dear?" she said to Marlon's father.

"Hurruump grump," he said as he turned over on the couch.

"Great!" said Marlon. "Camp starts tomorrow."

Marlon was up with the sun. She ran to the kitchen and stuffed a piece of bread in her mouth. She shoved the camp papers in her pocket.

"See you later, Mom!" she called as she ran out the door.

"Have fun, dear," her mom called sleepily. "Listen to your counselor and follow all the rules."

Marlon ran to the pirates' cabin and handed Shark Bait the papers.

"Let's be off," he said. Marlon got in line behind Peg Leg and they marched off toward the far end of the lake.

"I want to hear yer singing, lass," Shark Bait said. "Any sea dog worth her salt sings on the way to a good day of pirating." So they taught her a sea chantey.

"We're buccaneers all,

We're mean through and through,

Best give us yer gold

And yer pocket watch, too,

'Carz if ye don't,

Ye'll be swimming the deep,

And sharks will be

The company ye'll keep!"

William said, "We're near the secret cove where we hide our ship. Them that sees her can never tell anyone where she is. It's the pirates' code."

Chapter Four

They turned a corner and climbed through a stand of tall pine trees. Marlon was amazed. There, before her in the sparkling water, was a magnificent pirate ship.

"Wow," said Marlon.

"Aye, she's a beauty, she is," said Peg Leg.

The ship was painted with red and black stripes. Cannons peeked out from holes in the sides. Tall wooden masts reached up to the sky. Marlon looked up at the skull and swords on the black flag that fluttered in the breeze.

"It's called the Jolly Roger," said William, "and

it's meant to strike fear into the hearts of them that sees it."

"Well, it's working," Marlon said nervously.

When they got onboard, Peg Leg gave Marlon her official pirate uniform.

"These here are yer britches and yer shirt," Peg Leg said. "Yer don't get any real daggers or a cutlass until ye're older. Yer might cut yerself."

"But that's not fair," Marlon said. "How will I fight? Aren't pirates supposed to board other ships and fight and steal all their loot . . . their gold and silver and jewels?"

"Ye'll have plenty of time fer treasure, lass," Peg Leg said. "First, ye be needing yer basic pirating skills. Besides, we save our fightin' lessons for our advanced pirating class."

Shark Bait taught her to swagger. Peg Leg taught her to spit overboard. Then they taught her how to swab the deck.

"Wait a minute," said Marlon. "Swabbing a deck isn't fun. I thought camp was supposed to be fun!"

William laughed. "Swab it, mate, or ye'll walk the plank!"

"I will not," Marlon said, stomping her foot, "and you can't make me!"

"That's enough of that, girl," William said. He turned and reached deep into a wooden chest. Marlon gulped. Her eyes grew as big as two teacups.

Chapter Five

"Now wait a minute, William," she said, "I'm sorry. I always get into trouble with my mom for arguing too much. . . ."

William pulled out a big . . . orange . . . LIFE PRESERVER! He carefully tied it around Marlon.

"There ye be, lass," he said. "Can't have ye disobeying orders. Now walk the plank."

Shark Bait, Peg Leg, and William marched behind Marlon.

"There's nothing more satisfying than watching a good plank walk." Peg Leg grinned.

Marlon wasn't so sure. She walked to the end

of the plank. She looked down into the lake. It seemed a long way down.

"Jump!" yelled Shark Bait.

Marlon held her nose and jumped off the plank. SPLASH! She kicked her legs and bobbed to the top.

"That was fun!" she yelled. "Come on in!"

Shark Bait and William did cannonballs off the plank. Peg Leg tried a dive, but did a belly flop instead.

"Argh, that do sting!" he said with tears welling up in his eyes. Shark Bait and William laughed. But Marlon didn't.

"Let's go fix some lunch, Peg Leg," she said. "That will make you feel better."

Marlon made tuna sandwiches and lemonade. William spread fish eggs on bread.

"Yuck," said Marlon, "that looks disgusting."

"That's more for me," said William as he

stuffed a big drippy piece in his mouth.

They sat on the deck in the sun and had a pic-nic. After lunch Marlon swabbed the deck while the pirates napped.

"This is a great camp," Marlon said. "I wish that old Carla Axelrod could see me now."

Chapter Six

The next day William taught her how to climb up to the crow's nest.

"Nah, ye're too slow, girl!" he called. "Scamper on up! Yer need to be quick to spot the enemy's ship!"

Marlon kept chanting, "Don't look down, don't look down." Her knees were shaking. Her hands were sweaty. Her heart was beating hard. When she got to the top, she sat down in the nest. Slowly she sat up and peeked over the side.

"It's beautiful!" she said. "I can see the whole lake! I did it!"

William made Marlon practice climbing to the crow's nest over and over.

"That's a girl!" he said to her one day. "Ye're almost as fast as me. Ye'll be a fine spotter."

Marlon was proud.

By the end of the first week of camp, Marlon had learned lots of pirating skills.

Shark Bait taught her how to count treasure.

"We're fresh out of real treasure," said Shark Bait. "But this here penny jar of William's will do." He gave the jar to Marlon.

"One . . . two . . . ," said Marlon as she dropped pennies into a wooden chest.

"Count them faster, lass!" said Shark Bait. "And by Blue Beard's big toe, look over yer shoulder now and then! Or some ugly pirate might snatch himself some of yer loot."

Peg Leg made her practice boarding an enemy ship.

"Climb up that mast, grab that rope, and swing across!" he said. "Over there!"

He pointed to a small rowboat in the water next to the pirate ship.

"It's not much," he said. "But it's all we have. If yer can land on that, yer can land on anything."

"But that's just stupid," said Marlon. "Why don't I just swim over and climb onboard?"

"Aye, that's a fine idea as well. We'll save that fer tomorrow. But today ye're swinging over to that there boat. 'Carz sometimes ye'll have to board another ship and do battle," he said.

"Now climb the mast and grab that rope. Then just swing across. And hurry, lass! Yer don't want the enemy to board our ship first!"

Marlon climbed a little ways up the mast. She grabbed the rope with both hands. She pushed off the mast with her feet. Marlon could see dark blue water below her. Then she saw the rowboat.

She squeezed her eyes shut. "Now!" she thought. But she couldn't let go.

"I can't do it!" she yelled. Marlon held tight to the rope. She swung back and forth. Just like a pendulum on a clock. Finally she stopped swinging. She opened her eyes and dropped to the deck. Right in front of Peg Leg.

"That'll never do, lass." He frowned. "Shinny on back up and do it again!"

Marlon climbed back up and grabbed the rope. "Stupid rowboat," she grumbled. She pushed harder off the mast. She swung out over the water. "Ready or not, here I come!" she yelled. She forced herself to keep her eyes open.

"Let go!" yelled Peg Leg. Marlon let go and landed. Right in the water. The rowboat bobbed peacefully next to her.

Dripping, Marlon came up to the deck. She marched over to the rope and grabbed it. She stared at the rowboat in the water.

"This time," she said to Peg Leg, "I'm going to nail it."

Marlon climbed up. She pushed off. She looked down. There it was, right there.

"Cowabunga!" she yelled as she let go of the rope. Marlon landed smack in the middle of the rowboat.

"That's it!" yelled Peg Leg. "That's the spirit!"

"That might be the spirit!" Marlon yelled back. "But my bottom is bruised!"

CHAPTER SEVEN

As the days passed, Marlon got to know the pirates better. The pirates didn't care if she burped after she ate. In fact, they slapped her on the back and laughed. The pirates didn't take baths or comb their hair. They never made fun of her name or the way she looked. And they never used a napkin to wipe the peanut butter and jelly off their faces.

"Aye, mate, what der ye think that shirt of yers is for?" said Shark Bait as he smeared peanut butter across his beard.

Marlon liked the pirates. It seemed to her that the pirates liked her, too. And she knew they were starting to trust her. Because on the second week of camp they decided to teach her how to sail the pirate ship.

"Can I take her out to the middle of the lake?" said Marlon.

"Nar," said Shark Bait. "Ye're not ready yet. Can't have ye plowing this fine beauty into the side of another ship. Ye'll stay in the bay for a bit. We'll see how ye do. Before we turn ye loose in deeper water."

Marlon loved being at the helm. She sailed around and around the bay. Finally the pirates let Marlon sail out of the bay and into the lake. She headed right for the cluster of cabins on the other side.

"Ahoy there!" Marlon called to her mom as they sailed by. But her nose was buried in her book. Her mom raised her arm and waved in Marlon's direction.

"Avast ye, matey!" Marlon yelled to her dad. He was stretched out in the hammock on the dock. Marlon could hear his snores bounce off the ship's sides.

CHAPTER EIGHT

Marlon and the pirates sailed, fished, and swam every day.

In the afternoons they would stretch out on the deck. The pirates would tell her stories.

Peg Leg told her about his favorite parrot, Slim Jim.

"Slim Jim weren't just any parrot, lass," said Peg Leg. "He was as sharp as a dagger. And he could read. He read from sunup to sundown. His favorite thing to read was cookbooks."

Peg Leg looked off into the distance. He shook his head a little. "I bought that bird every cookbook from Australia to Zanzibar. But it weren't enough. That bird took off one day for Paris, France. Never a word. Well, sure, he left me a note. But that's not the same as a proper good-bye."

Peg Leg wiped a tear from his eye. "Now Slim Jim works at a fancy French hotel. Reads the chef his recipes. Samples all the dishes. Gets paid handsomely, from what I hear."

"Wow," said Marlon.

William told her about becoming a pirate.

"Well, it was a sorry excuse for a pirate child-hood, it was. I was born into a nice enough family. They wore clean clothes and had good manners. Three meals a day. A bath every night. A soft bed. Never even one twitch of adventure." William shuddered.

"Aye, me parents knew I wasn't happy. So they shipped me off to my uncle Ulysses. He taught me everything I know about pirating. Shark Bait here was his first mate.

"We sailed the world over. Then one day . . . a Tuesday, I think it was, Uncle Ulysses decided to go ashore. 'I've had enough water,' he said. So he found himself an island. Only ten people on the whole thing. And Uncle Ulysses made him-self their king."

"Wow," Marlon said again.

"Aye, and he had four pet monkeys last time I saw him," said William.

Shark Bait told her about the pirates he had sailed with and the adventures they had.

He told her about Pink Nose Pete, Jellyfish Jake, and Limping Larry.

"Them was the best no-good bunch of pirates ever was," he said.

"Um, Shark Bait," said Marlon. "Was there a pirate on the ship that you *didn't* like?" Marlon thought about Carla Axelrod calling her names on the playground.

Shark Bait snorted. "There was one scoundrel. A beast of a pirate. As mean and nasty as a barracuda with a bad tooth. Name of Toothless Tom. Never gave me a moment's peace. Followed me around day and night. I could never do anything right in his eyes."

Marlon couldn't believe it. Who would pick on

Shark Bait? To Marlon, he looked like the fiercest pirate in the world.

"What did he do to you?" she said.

"Argh," said Shark Bait. "Tormented me, he did. Laughed at the way I tied knots. Made fun of me hook. Said the shark got the smartest part of me." Shark Bait nodded his head. "Aye, he was a right big pain."

"What happened? How did you get rid of him? Did you throw him overboard in the night?" said Marlon hopefully.

Shark Bait laughed. "I thought about it many times," he said. "But no, lass. Can't be throwing yer crewmates over the side. Captain wouldn't approve. No, Toothless Tom just got sick of me."

"Oh," she said sadly. Marlon didn't think Carla Axelrod would *ever* get sick of her.

CHAPTER NINE

The last week of camp was Marlon's happiest. She spent the mornings sailing and practicing her pirating skills. In the afternoons they played cards and ate ice cream. Marlon felt right at home with the pirates. But all too soon the week was over.

"Well, lass, our time together is done," said Shark Bait. "Tomorrow we'll have our Pirate Graduation Party and send ye on yer way. Ye've learned all we could teach ye, and ye've learned it well."

Peg Leg said, "Aye, it's true. Wee Marlon's got the pirate spirit."

Marlon thought the pirate party was fantastic. She danced a jig while the pirates sang. William timed her climbing up to the crow's nest.

"Ye've beaten your best time!" he said.

Shark Bait and William made a cheese pizza just for her. The pirates ate pickled herring and dried fish with crackers.

Peg Leg floated a watermelon in the lake to get it cold. They fished it out with a net and sliced it on the deck. The juice ran down the fronts of their shirts. They had a contest to see who could spit a seed the farthest. Marlon won.

Then it was time for Marlon to leave.

"May yer sails always be full," Shark Bait said as he dabbed at the corners of his eyes with his sleeve.

"May the sharks never nibble yer toes," said William as he choked back a sob.

"May yer coffers be full and yer ship never

leak," said Peg Leg as he hugged Marlon.

"I'll miss you all," Marlon said. "Camp Buccaneer is the best thing that ever happened to me. I hope I get to see you again."

"Ye never know when our paths will cross," said Shark Bait as he handed Marlon a box. Inside was a Jolly Roger, just like the one that flew over the pirate ship.

"And if ye ever need us, fer any reason . . . like the enemy's coming fer yer ship, or ye're down to yer last doubloon, just hoist this up yer flag-pole, lass."

"This is so great!" Marlon said. Tears filled her eyes. She quickly wiped them away.

"Thanks, you guys," Marlon said. "I guess I'm a real pirate now."

"Aye, ye're one of us, lass," William said.

CHAPTER TEN

Marlon's family went back to the city the next day and before she knew it, school was starting.

On the first day of school, Marlon had all the fingers on both of her hands crossed.

She chanted, "Please no Carla Axelrod," over and over in her head.

But when Marlon got to her classroom, there she was. When Carla saw Marlon, her eyes lit up with glee and she smiled a wicked smile.

"She's happy because she gets to torture me for another year," Marlon thought.

Marlon's teacher, Mrs. Miller, said, "Class, I

want you to sit in alphabetical order. The first row is Alex Ace, then Marlon Adams, then Carla Axelrod . . ."

"I should have changed my name to Zadams," thought Marlon. "I guess it's too late now."

But when class started, a wonderful thing happened. Mrs. Miller said, "Class, I want you each to write an essay about your summer vacation."

Marlon was so happy. "I know just what to say. I'll tell them all about the pirates," she thought.

She wrote a great essay. When Mrs. Miller called her name to read, Marlon was proud. She told them about the pirates. She told them about walking the plank and sailing on the lake. She told them about learning to climb up to the crow's nest. When she was done, the class was very quiet.

CHAPTER ELEVEN

"Marlon, perhaps you misunderstood," said Mrs. Miller. "I wanted you to write something that REALLY did happen this summer."

"Good job, Mush Mouth," Carla snickered behind her.

"But, Mrs. Miller," said Marlon, "I *did* go to Camp Buccaneer. They were *real* pirates."

Carla giggled. Marlon felt her cheeks turning red.

Mrs. Miller said, "Well, Marlon, I can see that you have a very active imagination. Let's see, who is next? Carla, would you read us your paper?"

At the end of the day Mrs. Miller said, "Since

we are just getting to know each other, I want you to bring in something that is special to you. Then we'll take turns talking about them."

"Maybe Marlon can bring in one of her great, big pirate friends," Carla whispered. Marlon heard the class snicker behind her.

"Another great year at school," Marlon said to herself.

She didn't feel like eating dinner that night.

"Are you sick, sweetie?" her mom said as she flipped through a magazine.

"Yeah, I have Carla Axelroditis," Marlon said as she went out the back door.

Marlon sat on the back porch and thought about the "special thing" she was supposed to bring to class.

"The problem is," Marlon thought, "there's really nothing special about me. Except that I'm a pirate, and nobody believes that."

Marlon looked up at the tall flagpole that her dad had put up on the last Fourth of July.

"Hey, it's worth a try!" Marlon said as she dashed back into the house and up to her room.

"Dad, can I use the flagpole until tomorrow?" Marlon asked.

"What? Use it for what?" her dad asked as he clicked the remote control.

"To hoist my Jolly Roger. I need the pirates to come so I can share them at school," she said.

"Sure, honey," he said. "Could you move out of the way? I can't see my game."

Marlon ran out the back and raised the Jolly Roger.

"Maybe," she said as she watched it wave in the breeze, "just maybe, they'll see it."

CHAPTER TWELVE

Marlon hopped out of bed the next day and ran out to her front yard. She looked up and down the street. No pirates. She got dressed for school and got on the bus. No pirates.

As the bus doors closed, Marlon thought, "Well, I guess that was a pretty stupid thing to do. It's not like Shark Bait, Peg Leg, and William can see my house from the lake."

After lunch Mrs. Miller said, "All right, class, it's time for us to share our special things that we brought from home. Alex, you are first."

Alex shared a rock that came from a volcano.

"Marlon, do you have anything to share with us?" Mrs. Miller asked.

"Well . . ." started Marlon.

Just then there was a knock at the door. When Mrs. Miller opened it, her jaw dropped. Her hands flew up to her cheeks. There, standing in the doorway, was Shark Bait, dressed in his best britches and shirt. A red sash was tied around his waist and his cutlass was lashed to his side.

"Beg pardon, missus," Shark Bait said as he pushed his way in. "We be looking for a fellow pirate that goes by the name of Marlon."

Marlon jumped up.

"Here I am, Shark Bait!" she said.

Peg Leg and William came over to her desk.

"We came as soon as we got yer signal. Which of these varmints do we tie to the mast?" Peg Leg said. "Or maybe it's all of the little demons!"

"Aye, there may be only three of us, but we're

three they'll never forget!" William growled at the class.

"No, it's okay!" said Marlon. "I just wanted you to tell them that I really am a pirate!"

"Shiver me timbers!" Shark Bait said. "We forgot to give ye yer card, that says ye're a real pirate and all!"

He handed Marlon a card. It said:

THIS HERE ☒ GIRL ☐ BOY NAMED
MARLON
is a PIRATE, having finished Pirate training at Camp Buccaneer. Her pirate name will forever be:
MAD DOG MARLON

CAMP BUCCANEER

OFFICIAL SEAL

Signed,
X   X   X
SHARK BAIT   PEG LEG   WILLIAM

Mrs. Miller finally closed her mouth. When she opened it again, she said, "I have never met a real pirate before." She stared at Shark Bait, William, and Peg Leg. Then she suddenly clapped her hands together.

"I have an idea!" Mrs. Miller said. "Our class will be studying cultures from around the world. Would you please stay and speak to the class about life on the high seas?"

"It would be a pleasure, missus," said Shark Bait.

They told the class about pirate life. Marlon taught the class how to dance a jig. She decided *not* to show them how to spit.

"That can wait for recess," she thought.

The very last thing Marlon taught them was her sea chantey.

"Although I am small
And I flunk my math tests,

I can sail, spit, and swagger

Along with the best,

My looks might be poor,

But I'm rich in my spirit,

And if *you* don't like me,

I don't want to hear it."

The class clapped loudly when she finished singing. Marlon took a deep bow.

CHAPTER THIRTEEN

After school Carla Axelrod came up to Marlon.

"Hey, Marlon, these pirate guys are pretty cool," she said. "I was wondering if you could talk them into coming to my birthday party. Oh . . . and I guess you can come, too."

"Gee, Carla," said Marlon, "I don't think real pirates have time for birthday parties. We're too busy looking for bullies to feed to the sharks."

Carla looked at Marlon. She looked over at Shark Bait, William, and Peg Leg. Then she turned and ran.

Marlon said, "Come on, you guys have to meet my parents. Maybe you can stay for dinner!"

Marlon and the pirates walked all the way to her house. When her neighbors saw Marlon and the three pirates walking down the street, they went in their houses and shut their doors.

When Marlon got home, she yelled, "Mom, Dad, where are you? I brought the pirates home to meet you!"

"That's nice, dear," her mom said. "I'm in the den with your father!"

Marlon walked in the den. Her mom was sitting on the couch, buried in a book. Her dad was sitting next to her mom, staring at the TV.

"So, Mom, Dad, these are the pirates from Camp Buccaneer," Marlon said. "Have a seat on the couch, William. You too, Peg Leg. Shark Bait and I will sit over here."

"So, ye're Mad Dog Marlon's mother, are ye?"

William said as he plopped down on the couch next to her.

"And ye're making us some grub? Aren't that lovely? We're hungrier than a pack of pirates lost at sea fer forty weeks," said Peg Leg as he crashed down between her mom and dad. He flung his feet up on the coffee table with a THUD.

Marlon's mom looked at Peg Leg. Then she turned and looked at William.

"P . . . ppp . . . pi . . . rates . . . ," she stuttered. "HELP! Run, Marlon, RUN!" She jumped up from the couch. Her book flew across the room and landed on Shark Bait's toe.

"Youch!" he scowled. "Be a mite more careful where ye launch them things!"

Her dad's eyes moved slowly from the TV to Shark Bait's face.

"Oh, my," he said as he dropped the remote control.

"Hey, Mom, Dad, relax!" said Marlon. "These are the pirates from Camp Buccaneer. You remember, I told you all about them."

Marlon introduced everyone.

"Oh, of course, I just didn't realize that . . . you were . . . um . . . er . . . real . . . ," Marlon's mom said.

"Can they stay for dinner, Mom?" Marlon asked.

"Well, of course they can," her mom said. "Let's see, tonight we're having Tuna Surprise."

"Argh, a tasty fish dish, no doubt," William said, rubbing his stomach.

Her dad stood up and turned off the TV.

"You know," he said, "I always wanted to be a pirate when I was a boy." He stared jealously at Shark Bait's hook.

Marlon set the kitchen table, placing knives and forks at each setting.

"Guess what?" she whispered to her mom. "*Real* pirates don't use napkins."

The pirates ate three helpings of Tuna Surprise. They talked about the summer, and how Marlon had learned to be a card-carrying pirate. Marlon's mom and dad listened to every word, leaning over their plates and hardly touching their dinners.

When dinner was over, her dad said, "Shark Bait, do you think that you, Peg Leg, William, and . . . Mad Dog Marlon . . . could teach a couple of landlubbers like us to be *real* pirates?"

Shark Bait looked at Marlon, "What thinks ye, lass? Be they made of pirate stuff?"

Marlon smiled and said, "No problem, Mom and Dad."